The Lost Diary of Christopher Columbus's Lookout

The Lost Diary of Christopher Columbus's Lookout

Caught by Clive Dickinson
Illustrated by George Hollingworth

Collins

An imprint of HarperCollinsPublishers

First published in Great Britain by Collins 2000
Collins is an imprint of HarperCollins*Publishers* Ltd
77–85 Fulham Palace Road, Hammersmith,
London, W6 8JB

The HarperCollins website address is:
www.**fire**and**water**.com

1 3 5 7 9 8 6 4 2

Text copyright © Clive Dickinson 2000
Illustrations by George Hollingworth 2000

ISBN 0 00 694596-1

The author and illustrator assert the moral right
to be identified as the author and illustrator of this work.

Printed and bound in Great Britain by
Omnia Books Limited, Glasgow

MESSAGE TO READERS

It isn't very often that unknown records of famous events in history are discovered by accident. However, this is exactly what happened when Clive Dickinson caught something much fishier than a fish on a recent weekend fishing trip.

After trawling up several old boots and a couple of sprats, Clive pulled a small wooden barrel out of the water. Inside were pages of rough paper, smelling faintly of tobacco and covered in childlike sketches of what seemed like life on a desert island. There was writing too – in Spanish – and, from Mr Dickinson's rudimentary knowledge of this language from his frequent holidays in Spain, it seemed to describe a sea journey.

Mr Dickinson soon discovered that he had a priceless document in his hands. Although the name Christopher Columbus* did not appear on any of the pages, it was clear that the writing described the famous voyage Columbus led in 1492, across the Atlantic Ocean, to discover a new sea route to Asia.

Christopher Columbus had kept his own day-by-day account of the voyage, but his original journal has been lost over the last 500 years. Could this new discovery be the only surviving record of that great event?

Using the Internet, Mr Dickinson found two experts on medieval voyages who agreed to examine his find (for a very reasonable price, he says). Dr Miles Away, an Alaskan academic, and the Spanish historian Don Believavor D'Ovid confirmed that the pages in the leather folder were indeed written in 1492 by a member of Columbus's expedition, who sailed with him on the flagship, the *Santa Maria*. His duties are a little unclear, but he appears to have spent some of his time as a lookout.

Now, after five centuries, extracts from this remarkable first-hand account have been translated and can be published, recording one of the great turning points in world history, when the Old World and the New World met for the first time.

* *'Columbus' is a Latin version of the discoverer's name, which was written differently at various times of his life, depending on the country in which he was living. In Genoa and Portugal he was called Colombo. In Spain his name was written Colón. It is unlikely he ever knew himself by the English name, Christopher Columbus.*

1 April 1492 – *Toledo, central Spain*

¡Ay caramba! I still can't believe what's happened.

There are only eight years to go until the start of the new century and people are already getting worked up about it. Some are predicting that the world's going to end and that none of us will ever see the year 1500.

No-one in our household expected anything like this, though. If it wasn't so serious, I'd think someone was playing a huge April Fool joke on everyone in Spain. But this isn't a joke – it's for real. We heard the news yesterday. There was a Royal Proclamation from the King and Queen and you don't mess around with orders from the top.

King Ferdinand and Queen Isabella have commanded every Jew to leave Spain by the beginning of August. The only ones allowed to stay are Jews who give up being Jews and change their religion to become Christians.

I can't see my old master, Isaac Palestino, doing that. After what he's told me about the Jewish people – how all through their history they've been kicked out of one country after another – I expect he'll pack up, leave Spain and find a new home over the sea.

We've been waving goodbye to the Muslims recently. For hundreds of years, Muslim rulers had their own kingdom down in the south of the country. Then, three months ago, on 2 January this Year of Our Lord 1492, the great city of Granada itself surrendered to our King and Queen. That's a date for the history books. For the first time in centuries, Spain is one country again – a Christian country.

The last of the Muslims have left. Now all the Jews are going. What will be next? They say things happen in threes and if there isn't a third amazing event in the wind this year, my name isn't Luc Landahoya.

2 April 1492 – *Toledo, central Spain*

Master Isaac called me into his study yesterday to break the news that I'll be out of a job. He's been so good to me, I was close to tears. He's taught me to read. I can write. I know a bit of Latin. And I must know more about the world outside Spain than any other servant in the kingdom. When I think about the hours I've spent in that study, surrounded by his books, listening to him talking about the great thinkers of ancient times, hearing about the amazing places people have travelled to, I can't believe that's all coming to an end – and so suddenly.

Master Isaac told me that he's going to take the family to the land of the Moors in North Africa. Apparently he's got relatives there.

After what's happened down in Granada, I don't think a Christian like me would be too welcome in the land of the Moors. But I don't want to stay in Toledo. Life wouldn't be the same. I fancy a change. Perhaps I'll try my luck in another country.

13 May 1492 – *Palos, south-west Spain*

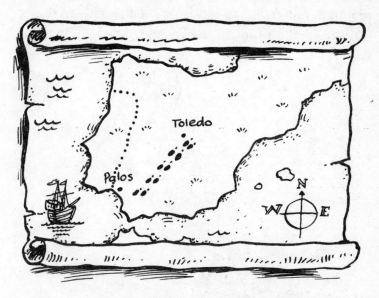

I got here a couple of days ago. Palos wasn't top of my list of Spain's seaside towns. I was going to travel to a big exciting port like Seville or Cadiz.

Then I found out that all the big ports were crammed full of people like my old master and his family, looking for ships to take them overseas. I could see that I'd be stuck for months, waiting at the back of the queue for all the Jews to leave, before I found a place on a ship. Master Isaac suggested that I should try somewhere smaller. Palos isn't as popular as Seville or Cadiz. You don't get many rich people coming down to this little town beside the Tinto River. But the weather's warm and sunny and there are ships here. It's close to Portugal. And it's a good place from which to sail to Mediterranean lands or northwards to countries like France, or Holland, or even England.

I've found somewhere to stay in the monastery of La Rabida and I reckon I'll find what I'm looking for before too long.

23 May 1492 – *Palos*

Today there was another command from King Ferdinand and Queen Isabella. This was a special letter from Their Majesties to the people of Palos! The town clerk read it aloud in the Church of St George, where all the important people of the town had gathered. I didn't think it would be of much interest to me, since I'm only passing through. But I went along to find out what was going on, and *hombre*, am I glad I did!

It seems that some fellow from the state of Genoa, across the sea in the land of Italy, has persuaded the King and Queen to put up the money for a special voyage. The King and Queen have given this Genoese sailor the rank of Captain General and they say he's going to sail in three ships to certain parts of the Ocean Sea*. Call me Luc Landlubba, but that makes no sense! How can one man sail three ships at once?

It sounds sort of secret (not to mention magical), so it should be exciting. I pricked up my ears, though nobody else was that thrilled. You see, the proclamation also says that because the people of Palos have been breaking the law by trading along the North African coast and upsetting the King of Portugal, they've got to provide this Cristobál Colón** (I think that's the Captain General's name) with two ships and all the food and equipment needed for a voyage lasting a year.

* *Atlantic Ocean*   ** *Christopher Columbus*

They've got to have the ships and everything else ready in ten days' time. No wonder the locals are fed up about it.

The proclamation doesn't make it clear where this Colón fellow is going. All it says is that he must not go southwards to the African lands, which the King of Portugal claims are his. That only leaves two directions to sail across the Ocean Sea – north and west. Either way, this could be the chance I've been waiting for!

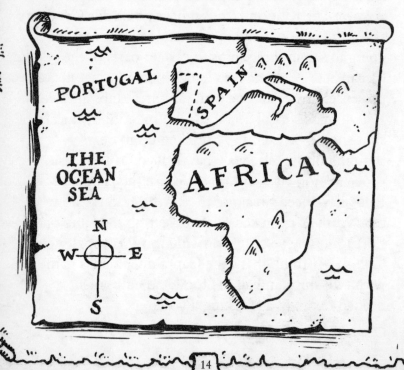

25 May 1492 – *Palos*

Two days ago I was really excited about the news in the Royal Proclamation.

Now I'm not so sure.

All over Palos, people are talking about it. From what I've heard, Captain General Cristobál Colón has been banging on about this voyage for ages. It seems that he's come up with a brand new way of reaching the Indies – the place where all our spices come from, not to mention expensive goods like silk and precious stones. Some say that he was here in Palos several years ago. By then he'd already tried to get the King of Portugal to pay for his expedition, but Portuguese experts told the King to save his money.

Of course he isn't the only one to have these big ideas. For a long time sailors from over the border in Portugal have been exploring down the coast of Africa. Until four years ago, all they did was keep sailing southwards. They reckon that if they keep going, *they'll* find a new route to the Indies. But it wasn't much use, because to get to the Indies you have to go eastwards. That was one of the first things I learned from Master Isaac. So I guess the Portuguese are going to be sailing forever.

But four years ago, in 1488, Bartolomeu* Dias sailed back to Portugal with earth-shattering news. He'd discovered the bottom end of Africa, the southern tip, where the land stops and our Ocean Sea carries on round into another stretch of water, which must lead to the Indies.

* *Bartholomew in English*

If he's right, the Portuguese have discovered how to sail to the distant lands of Asia – the Indies. But having to sail right round Africa to get there will make it an awfully long trip – and however long would it take to get back?

Captain General Colón's idea couldn't be more different. Perhaps that's why so few people take him seriously. After being turned down by the King of Portugal, he took his plan to our King and Queen.

This was six years ago, in 1486. He told them that he'd worked out how he could cut down the distance to the lands of Asia by sailing *westwards*! The man must be mad!

It sounds daft, but he must have done some clever talking, because Their Majesties ordered a group of Spanish experts to look at the plan. But the experts turned down the idea just like the Portuguese. I heard somewhere that the Captain General had fiddled the distances to make Asia look closer to Spain than it really is.

Who's to say who's right? No-one knows what lies over the horizon. There are still a few people who think the earth's flat and that you'll fall off the edge if you sail too far in any direction! At least most people now know that's a crazy idea.

In Master Isaac's library I read books which describe terrible monsters out beyond the Ocean Sea. Then there are those stories about sailors from lands in the far north – where the Vikings lived back in the last millennium – that tell of sailing westwards and finding land.

I also read about a holy man from Ireland who did the same thing. St Brendan was supposed to have sailed away in a boat made of leather, to find land to the west.

Who are they trying to kid? That was over 500 years ago, and what do you hear of Vikings, St Brendan or those lands now? Nothing. I can see why so many experts don't believe in the Captain General's plan.

But the King and Queen must have believed him, because Colón's got his money and his ships. This could be the change of scene that I wanted. I am going to see what more I can find out...

15 June 1492 – *Palos*

The Captain General is having a hard time with his 'Enterprise of the Indies', as it's called. People are making fun of him openly in the streets.

Down the river, two small ships* are being made ready for him, but what use are ships without sailors? And the Captain General can't find anyone to sail with him.

The King and Queen have offered to let men out of prison if they sign up for the trip, but even the prisoners don't seem that keen.

They've also promised to pay the men who go with the Captain General with their own Royal money. It looks as if the sailor from Genoa will be on the move again if he can't find his crews. I don't want to be the only one to put my name down for this voyage into the unknown – however exciting it might sound to me.

known as 'caravels'

22 June 1492 – *Palos*

I had a very interesting talk with one of the friars at my lodgings in the monastery last night. He told me that another friar, Antonio de Marchena, had helped the Captain General when he went to see the King and Queen about his Enterprise of the Indies.

Friar Antonio is one of the wisest men in Spain. It seems that he was also one of the first to take the Captain General's plan seriously, and he put in a good word for Colón when he was called to explain his idea to Their Majesties.

Now he's helping again. Thanks to Friar Antonio, Martin Alonso Pinzon is going to join the expedition. Martin Alonso is probably the most important sea captain in Palos. He was away when the Royal Proclamation was read. Now he's back in town, Friar Antonio must have advised him to get his name down for the voyage, before he misses the chance. If he joins the Captain General, other sailors in Palos will be sure to sign up too.

I'd better get down to the Captain General's first thing in the morning.

23 June 1492 – *Palos*

There's now a rush of people wanting to sign up for the voyage. No-one wants to miss the boat! It's because Martin Alonso Pinzon is going to be captain of one of the ships anchored in the river, the *Pinta*. Better still, he's got two of his brothers and a cousin to join the Captain General. One of his brothers is going to be captain of the other ship from Palos, the one they call the *Niña*. So no magical dividing-into-three from the Captain General, then. Shame. I'd like to have seen that, though I can't say I'd have liked being captained by just a pair of legs.

It was touch and go for me, because most of the men here have been sailing on ships all their lives. But the Captain General spotted me reading a notice about the voyage, and that clinched it. I don't think many of the others can read or write.

There's Luis de Torres, who speaks Arabic and several other languages. He's going along as interpreter. There are a couple of men from court sent by the King and Queen. Apart from them, most of the crew are sailors from up and down the coast.

The Captain General told me he could do with a lad with quick wits and sharp eyes on his flagship, the biggest of the three, which they've called the *Santa Maria*. Then he took me to one side and asked secretively, "Have you heard of Cathay* and the lands of the Great Khan?"

"You don't mean the lands where that traveller from Venice, Marco Polo, went 200 years ago?"

The Captain General put his fingers to his lips and winked. "His book has been a bestseller for a couple of centuries," he whispered. "But just wait till *mine* hits the streets." And he smiled knowingly.

* China

The strange thing is, I can't find anything written down to say that's where we're heading. No-one else seems to know exactly where he's taking us. But when the King and Queen give you an all-expenses-paid trip, you don't argue.

I kept the notice about the voyage. I've a hunch it might be useful one day.

Come along with Colón and see the world!
Attention Mariners!
Take a voyage of a lifetime. Sail beyond the Horizon and discover new lands.
All expenses paid, by Royal Command.
Your chance to grab a place in history before the century ends!

(Applicants must be prepared to sail away for a year and a day (or longer) to the land where the bong tree grows and other unknown places across the Ocean Sea. Captain General Colón and Their Majesties take no responsibility for bringing applicants home. Applicants must supply their own clothing and utensils. No berths aboard ship may be reserved. Fishing allowed. Swimming in the Ocean Sea by permission only. Only experienced mariners may steer the ships. The decision of the Captain General is final, even when he is wrong. List of successful applicants available to those who can read.)

23 July 1492 – *Palos*

This last month has gone in a flash. I'm still sleeping in the monastery at night, but during the day I'm down at the river helping to get ready for the voyage.

My main job has been writing down details about the crews. We've got about forty men on board the flagship, the *Santa Maria*. It's hard to keep track because among the crew are eleven Juans and four Diegos, Pedros and Rodrigos.

There are seven Juans aboard the *Pinta* with Captain Martin Alonso Pinzon. Altogether I make it twenty-six for the crew of the *Pinta*.

The *Niña* has got around twenty men. The captain is Vicente Yanez Pinzon. He's only got four Juans in his crew.

Since I've never been a sailor, I can't help much with the ropes and sails and things, so once we're at sea I'm going to be up in the rigging as a lookout. Why couldn't I have been christened with a safer name, like Luc Havsumviña?

The ships were a bit of a shock when I first saw them. They seem so *small*. No wonder they disappear from sight so quickly when they sail away from land. The Captain General has got a little cabin for himself at the back of the *Santa Maria*, but there's no proper shelter for the rest of us. We're going to have to sleep on the open deck, which won't be much fun. For one thing, the deck is curved, so you keep rolling down to the edge where the waves break over you.

And, in this hot weather, the black pitch painted over the wood turns all soft and sticky and gets between your toes, and all over your clothes and hands. But we need the dry space under the decks for our food and fresh water, so there's no point in moaning.

30 July 1492 – *Palos*

We've been loading food and other supplies on to the ships all this week. It can't be long now before we set off. Today, big wooden barrels full of wine were stored in the hold in the bottom of the ship. There are more barrels filled with food down below too. These supplies have got to last us a year, so Domingo Vizcaino, the cooper who looks after the barrels, is going to be busy making sure they don't leak. If they do, the food will spoil and then we'll be in trouble. The sailors say food on ships doesn't taste too good at the best of times. When it turns bad, it adds a whole new meaning to seasickness.

The Captain General had me checking that we had everything we needed as it came aboard, and I've got to take good care of the list. For some reason he has his suspicions about the supplies we are being given by the people of Palos.

PALOS·PROVISIONS

'Ever Serve You Right'

Expedition Eatables and Sailor's Store

Visit our website: palprov@weevil.com.

FRUITS & VEGETABLES

Almonds
Beans (dried)
chick peas (dried)
Garlic (not dried)
Lentils (dried)
Olives (in olive oil)
Raisins (dried, because that's what raisins are - partly dried grapes, stupid)
Rice (not dried any more than rice is normally dried, because rice is normally a

~Fish~

Anchovies (salted) Cod (dried and salted)
Fresh fish (you must be joking - catch your own, smarty pants) Sardines (salted)

MEAT

Beef (salted and pickled)

Fresh meat (see Fresh fish, above - though I don't suppose you'll catch many rabbits at sea)

Pork (salted and pickled)

OILS & STICKY THINGS

Honey
Molasses
Olive oil

Olive

OTHER DRIED THINGS

Flour   Sea biscuits

WET THINGS

Water
Wine

The sailors may not think much of food at sea, but looking at all those goodies, nuts and flour and raisins, it could be a piece of cake.

Also stored in the hold are all the spare ropes and sails, lanterns and candles, big cooking pots, fire irons and fishing tackle.

All we need now is the fresh water, which comes on board last. Once that's stowed away, everything will be ready.

1 August 1492 – *Palos (but not for much longer)*

We started loading the water today, fetching it from the well near the Church of St George, where we first heard about the voyage. The water was carried down to the river bank and tipped into the ship's boat until the boat was so full it was close to sinking. Then the boat was carefully rowed out to the ship, where the fresh water was scooped out with wooden buckets and tipped into the barrels in the hold.

I spent all day doing that and I'm exhausted. If the voyage is anything like as tiring, I'm in trouble – big time.

2 August 1492 – *aboard the* Santa Maria *in the Tinto River, Palos*

I'm still stiff from heaving buckets of water, but I don't suppose I'll mind far out in the Ocean Sea when it's the only fresh water to drink for hundreds, maybe *thousands* of miles (scary thought, that).

Today all three crews went to say prayers at a special church service in St George's. It's ten weeks since the Royal Proclamation and now we're all set to go. Everyone seems to have forgotten that we were supposed to have been ready in ten *days*.

After church I packed my bag in the monastery and said goodbye to the monks. "God be with you," said one of them, "I think you'll need him." It wasn't very encouraging.

"Don't forget to win new souls for Our Lord," shouted another as I walked out of the gate. He knew that the Captain General wants to turn any people we meet into Christians. He promised Queen Isabella that was one of his main reasons for the voyage.

But how many new Christians are we going to find in the lands of the Great Khan, if we do end up there? Marco Polo wrote that the people in Cathay are as civilized as we are in Europe. If that's right, I can't see them wanting to give up their religion, whatever it is. It's like my old master suddenly being asked to stop being Jewish and become Christian overnight. I can't work out what the Captain General's up to.

At the moment I must get used to living on the ship. My first night on board hasn't got off to a good start. The only flat places to sleep are on the hatches covering the hold and they were nabbed right away. At the moment I'm curled up beside the main mast, but I don't think I'll be getting much rest. We must sail with the outgoing tide, and that means leaving before sunrise tomorrow morning.

Where will I next touch dry land? What would Master Isaac think if he could see me? I hope he'd be pleased. I've been thinking about him a lot the last couple of days. Today was the last day for Jews to leave Spain. I wonder how he's getting on in his new world? I wonder how I'll get on in mine?

4 August 1492 – *somewhere at sea*

Our voyage started yesterday morning. Half an hour before sunrise, the order was given to raise the anchor. Some of the sailors used long oars to row the ships out to where the tide was strongest. Then there was the back-breaking work of hoisting the sails, so that the morning breeze could carry us out to sea.

It looks as if we'll be having one main meal a day, around eleven o'clock in the morning. This is cooked in a big pot heated over a firebox called a *fogon*. I was glad to see that sand is spread on the deck to stop it catching fire.

I expect I'll get used to the taste of salt meat, but I'm not sure about the sea biscuits. They're not like any biscuit I've ever eaten. For one thing they look and feel like a clay tile. You think your teeth will break when you try biting your first one.

Then I saw the sailors making their biscuits softer by soaking them in the stew we were eating. That makes them easier to chew, but I can think of a few dogs who would turn their noses up at them.

We've got over a ton of these biscuits on board, so it's not going to be a luxury cruise on the food front after all.

The sea is calm. At least that hasn't made me feel sick yet.

6 August 1492 – *somewhere else at sea*

Our ship, the *Santa Maria*, is the slowest of the three. The *Pinta* and the *Niña* are usually in front of us, only today there was trouble on board the *Pinta*, when the rudder, which steers the ship, broke loose. Captain Pinzon had it fixed quickly and the Captain General praised him for his good work, but I heard him muttering that some people in Palos had arranged for this to happen. He believes they want to stop him sailing to the Indies. He doesn't like the two Pinzon brothers getting in front of him all the time either. I can see trouble brewing.

9 August 1492 – *still at sea*

I couldn't work out why we've been sailing south, when all along the Captain General has been talking about finding a new way to the Indies by sailing west. Now everything has been explained. He's taking us to the Canary Islands, off the coast of Africa, and today we sighted the island they call Grand Canary. What a silly name!

Captain Pinzon has been ordered to repair the *Pinta* or find a new ship there. Meanwhile our ship and the *Niña* are sailing on to the island of Gomera. I've heard the crew whispering that the Captain General has a lady friend on Gomera. Others say they make good cheese on the island.

So it looks as if I'll be touching dry land sooner than I expected.

26 August 1492 – *Grand Canary*

We got the cheese, but the Captain General's lady friend wasn't at home. We hung about for twelve days, waiting for her to return. Then the Captain General decided to return to Grand Canary, to see how Captain Pinzon was getting on with his repairs, and (so I heard) because his lady friend turned out to be on Grand Canary all the time (guess you could call her his 'tweetheart', then!).

Only she wasn't there. She left harbour to sail back home a short time before we sailed in. The Captain General wasn't very pleased to hear that.

Captain Pinzon's only just arrived too. It took the *Pinta* two weeks to get into harbour. So he's feeling grumpy as well.

I'm beginning to see what people in Palos meant when they called this voyage a mystery tour. None of us know where we're going next.

28 August 1492 – *Grand Canary (still)*

Went sightseeing today.

The Captain General must have seen this poster too, because he's having a lot of work done "cheap" on the ships.

The *Pinta* is in the shipyard, being fitted with a new rudder. Her sails are being changed too, and so are the sails on the *Niña*. Now they'll both have square sails like the ones on the *Santa Maria*. According to the Captain General, the new sails will help the two ships sail better on the voyage, because he reckons the winds will now blow us westwards straight across the Ocean Sea to the

island of Cipangu*. A lot of the sailors think he's had the sails changed so that the Pinzon brothers don't race ahead and discover the Indies before him.

5 September 1492 – *Gomera (again)*

We're back here once more. All three ships arrived four days ago and the Captain General was in a much better mood when he finally met up with his lady friend.

We've filled up with more fresh water and taken on the last of our fresh meat and firewood. There's no turning back now. Tomorrow we set sail into the unknown.

* *Japan*

We've been given our sailing orders, which the Captain General made me write down as a record. The ships must stay in sight of each other and must meet up each day at dawn and at dusk for new orders (that will stop the Pinzons racing ahead). He says that we will find land 750 leagues* to the west, so we aren't to sail at night after we've gone 700 leagues.

The best part is that Queen Isabella is paying a huge reward – a year's pay every year, for the first man to sight land. "Look lively, Luc. You could be in luck," I said to myself.

10 September 1492 – *out on the Ocean Sea*

We lost sight of land today. The last landmark was the massive fiery mountain on Tenerife. Now that has disappeared below the horizon, we're on our own in the unknown.

News reached us that three Portuguese ships were lying in wait after we left the Canaries. (They're not the only ones suspicious about this voyage.) So we had to make a detour to avoid them. Now we're safe – from the Portuguese at any rate.

I'm not the only one to have a nervous feeling in my tummy. Even some of the old sailors didn't eat all their cooked sardines and olives. The Captain General was cheerful enough, telling us not to worry

* *a league equals about three miles*

and reminding us about the rich lands we're going to find. In Cipangu he says there are buildings with roofs covered in gold. He sounds so sure that's where we're heading, it makes me wonder if he knows more than he's letting on.

He's right about the winds. They've picked up now, and we're sailing so fast that waves are breaking over the front of the ship. I'm glad I'm not sleeping there.

At this rate we'll have sailed the 750 leagues to the Indies in no time at all. The Captain General told the crew we sailed forty-eight leagues today. The funny thing is that I'm sure I saw him writing sixty leagues when he was doing his sums. Does he know something we don't?

17 September 1492 – *somewhere on the Ocean Sea*

I suppose I should be pleased that the sea is calm and the winds keep blowing us westwards day after day.

What worries me is that the winds may *only* blow westwards. If they do, how are going to sail home again? Even *I* know you can't sail against the wind if it's blowing you backwards.

That's not my only concern. Last night the compass went wrong. When it was checked against the North Star, the compass needle was pointing slightly to the north-west. If the compass doesn't point north, we're in deep trouble.

The Captain General had the compass checked again just before dawn and this time the needle pointed straight at the North Star. He says the star moves, not the compass. I hope he's right.

25 September 1492 – *still somewhere on the Ocean Sea*

For the last ten days there have been signs of land. First there were land birds. Then loads of weed on the surface stretching in front of us like a huge carpet. We've seen whales, dolphins, and crabs walking on the seaweed, which the sailors say prove we must be close to land somewhere.

Three days ago Captain Pinzon asked the Captain General if he could look at his chart. Today he sent it back on a line between the two ships.

Captain Pinzon thinks there are islands in this part of the Ocean Sea and he wants to change course to find them. But the Captain General insists we keep heading west.

At sunset Captain Pinzon started yelling excitedly from the *Pinta* and pointing to the horizon. He was shouting that he could see land away to the south-west and wanted the Queen's reward.

The Captain General was so pleased I think he would have thrown the money across to him right away. I was up in the rigging, and sure enough, rising out of the sea was a long line about twenty-five leagues away. We all said a prayer of thanks to God and the Captain General changed course to sail south-west towards it.

The Indies, we've found them! History here I come.

26 September 1492 – *still on the Ocean Sea*

That land we saw was only cloud. We carry on sailing westwards.

1 October 1492 – *sailing westwards on the Ocean Sea (but for how much longer?)*

Today the Captain General told the crew that he and the pilot think we've sailed about 580 leagues from the Canary Islands. However, I know that he really thinks we've sailed more than 700 leagues.

If he's right, we must be close to the Indies – or  does he now think they're further away? Is he telling the crew we've sailed a shorter distance than we really have to stop them wanting to turn round and sail home?

6 October 1492 – *on the Ocean Sea (though I'm having doubts about even that now)*

We're all jumpy. It's almost a month since we set sail from the Canaries. Sailors are saying we've sailed at least 800 leagues, fifty leagues further than the Captain General told us before we left. Men are shouting "Land ho" more and more often.

Every time, they make me jump in case something's about to crash down on my head!

We still haven't found land, and the Captain General has threatened not to give the reward to anyone who shouts he's seen land but who's still wrong after three days.

I'm sick of sea biscuits. The meat is starting to smell as bad as it tastes. We catch fish for a treat and we have to drink more wine each day because the water is so disgusting.

Anyone who thought this expedition was going to be a picnic was seriously wrong – and yet the sailors tell me we're having a good voyage. What are the bad ones like, I want to know? Or maybe I *don't* want to know…

10 October 1492 – *sailing south-west on the Ocean Sea*

The Captain General changed course today. If he's so sure that Cipangu and the Indies are west of us, why are we going in a different direction? Is he lost? Has he been lost all along?

I'm so worried I find myself counting the time. Every half-hour I watch one of the ship's boys turn the big sand-glass upside down, so that the sand can run down into the bottom half for another thirty minutes. I want to be sure that they remember to turn that glass. It's our only way of knowing the time, and if they forget to turn it over, the navigation sums will go wrong and we shan't be able to work out where we are on the chart.

What really worries me is that someone may have forgotten to turn the glass earlier in the voyage. Perhaps we've been lost for weeks. Maybe we've sailed right past Cipangu? Maybe you can't sail westwards to the Indies after all?

Everyone except the Captain General feels the same. I hear sailors whispering about throwing him over the side and sailing home. The Captain General has heard them grumbling and has warned them that they won't escape punishment from the King and Queen even if they *do* drop him in the Ocean Sea. He's also reminded us about how rich we'll all be when we do reach the Indies (where have I heard that before?).

The other thing is that he's the only one who knows how to sail home again.

The plan now is that we will carry on sailing for three more days. If we still haven't found land, the Captain General has agreed that we can change course for home. In 144 turns of the sand-glass, we could be on our way back to the dear old world we know.

Why did I leave? If I ever meet Master Isaac again, I'll have something to say to him about his "big wide world"!

12 October 1492 – *very early morning, in the Indies!*

OK – I was beginning to have a few doubts. I'm the first to admit it. And if Master Isaac ever reads that bit above, I'll be happy to apologize to him.

As for the Captain General – sorry, the Admiral

of the Ocean Sea (the King and Queen promised him that rank if he discovered land to the west) – he looks as if he's just jumped over the moon.

It all started happening yesterday. There were the usual flights of birds, but I'd given up on them as a sure sign of land. Then sailors started picking up reeds, canes and bits of wood floating on the surface. One looked as if it had been carved by something with a sharp edge – a knife, perhaps?

At sunset the ships came together as usual, and this time the Admiral was really excited. He reminded everyone about the huge reward and said he'd add a doublet of silk to the Queen's money for the first man to sight land.

I climbed into the rigging and didn't get a wink of sleep. Some time before midnight I heard the Captain General talking to the two men from the Royal Court sent along on the voyage by Their Majesties. I overheard them discussing a faint light like a candle far away in the darkness.

The Captain General and one of the courtiers had seen this light. The other said he hadn't. I squinted into the night, but I couldn't decide by that time whether or not my eyes were playing tricks.

It was probably another false alarm – or so I thought.

About three hours later, my eyelids were starting to droop when I heard my name being called from the *Pinta*, which was sailing in front of us, as usual.

"Give it a break," I shouted back. "Don't you know what time it is?"

"Look! Land ho!" shouted the voice from the darkness again, followed immediately by the boom of a cannon – the signal that land really had been sighted!

That brought everyone to the side of the ship. At first I couldn't see anything different. Then a thin white line came into view two leagues from us – waves crashing on a beach.

It was Juan – sorry, one – of the Juans on the *Pinta* who saw land first, so he's won the reward and the silk doublet. But I'm not complaining. We've found the Indies by sailing west. We'll be famous for the rest of time!

12 October 1492 – *evening in the Indies*

It's been a funny sort of day, but I suppose that's what this discovery business is all about – dealing with the unexpected.

We lowered the sails and waited offshore until sunrise. After sailing all this way, it would have been a shame to have run on to rocks and sunk the ships.

As soon as it was light, the Admiral (the Captain General wants us to call him this now), the two Pinzon captains, the two men from the Royal Court, the fleet's lawyer and a couple of others rowed ashore in the *Santa Maria*'s boat. They carried the flag of the King and Queen and the flags of the three ships, and after erecting a wooden cross and saying a few prayers, the Admiral claimed the new land for Their Majesties – he has named it San Salvador.

What puzzles me is that if we've arrived in the same Asia where all our silks and precious stones and spices come from, it must belong to someone already. So why is the Admiral claiming it for our King and Queen?

An even bigger puzzle was waiting for us. While we were watching the Admiral and the others rowing towards the shore, a crowd of people were also watching them from the beach. Maybe they'd just been for a swim, or perhaps it's one of those special holiday camps where people walk about in the all-together. Whatever this place is, these people aren't what we expected to find, because none of them are wearing any clothes!

I've read Marco Polo's book about Asia and the land of the Great Khan from cover to cover, and he never mentions people not wearing clothes. I can't make it out.

On top of this, they don't seem to know anything about weapons. When one of them was shown a sword, he grabbed the sharp blade with his hand and seemed very surprised that he cut himself. Yet the land of the Great Khan is famous for its fine swords and other weapons.

However, the Admiral came back to the ship very pleased with himself. Apparently we've landed on an island. He says it's one of the islands off the mainland of Asia, which the natives call Guanahani. It seems that we must have sailed past the island of Cipangu and ended up here instead.

He didn't mention gold roofs and precious jewels, but something's going on, because he's claimed the Queen's reward for himself. Juan on the *Pinta* had a few things to say about this. Still, the Admiral is the Admiral, and if he reckons that

little light he saw last night was the first sighting of land, there's not much Juan can do about it.

Later in the day, many of the island people swam out to our ships bringing gifts. Cotton thread wound up in balls, spears, brightly-coloured feathers – the sort of things people usually buy on holiday. They also offered us bunches of dried leaves, which was pretty weird. Not as tacky as some souvenirs I've seen, but still.

My mate went to Guanahani and all I got was this lousy T-shirt!

Guanahani

New World Original

Brooch

Pot o potty price

In return we gave them coloured glass beads, the little bells that hunting hawks wear, and red caps. They thought these were brilliant. But after sailing all this way, we're hoping there's more than just spears and leaves on offer. We're hoping to find gold and the other precious things we get from Asia.

Still, this is only an island. The Admiral says we'll find what we're looking for when we get to the mainland.

13 October 1492 – *San Salvador*

I was worrying about this island all last night and then I twigged!

I know what this place is. I should have guessed sooner, because the only people here are young adults and teenagers. It's one of those holiday resorts for people under thirty! That must be why so many of them go round with their face and bodies painted black, red or white – it must be their way of preventing sunburn.

It's certainly a great place for a holiday – sunny, sandy, with crystal-clear water, beautiful green forests and all kinds of fruit I've never seen before.

As well as swimming, there are great watersports. They don't have boats like ours, using oars and sails. Their boats are long and narrow and look as if they've been hollowed out from tree trunks.

Some of their boats are only big enough to carry one or two people, while others are *massive*, with room for forty or fifty! They're all moved along in the same way, with paddles shaped like the ones a baker uses for taking bread out of a hot oven – and can they move! They'd leave all of our boats standing.

Even the Admiral is impressed with these boats, though he does seem more interested in finding gold. I don't think he'll have much luck on this island. The people I've seen only wear small bits of gold hanging from holes in their noses. Maybe they don't wear a lot of jewellery when they're on the beach.

NO JEWELLERY PERMITTED ON BEACH.

16 October 1492 – *at sea again*

I could tell the Admiral was getting itchy feet at San Salvador.

Yesterday he took the ship's boat along the coast to explore the island, but what he found looked just the same as the place where we landed: more warm clear water, golden beaches, tall green forests and handsome people running around with no clothes on.

One of the sailors said it reminded him of Paradise, and the people on the beaches must have been having similar thoughts, because some of them pointed to the Admiral and then pointed to the sky. They think we've dropped down from heaven.

Several 'Indians', as we have started calling them, are staying on board our ship. Not that they have much choice about sailing with us – the Admiral wants them to help him find his way to Cipangu and the mainland of Cathay.

They named over a hundred islands we could sail to, so the Admiral decided to head for the biggest. We went there yesterday, named it after the Virgin Mary, handed out more glass beads and hawks' bells to the Indians who met us (they don't any wear clothes either) and then sailed off again.

Today we overtook a man in a *canoa**, the wooden boat they paddle around in here. He was on his way to the same island as us (the Admiral is going to name this one after King Ferdinand). In his *canoa* he had a string of our beads and some small Spanish coins, which means he must have come from San Salvador.

He also had a bunch of the same sort of dried leaves we were given when we arrived. There must be something very special about them, because people keep presenting them to us. I can't think why. If you ask me, the only thing dried leaves are good for is going up in smoke.

* canoe

24 October 1492 – *at sea once more*

We've been 'discovering' islands all week and still the Admiral hasn't found Cipangu. For that matter he hasn't found any gold worth speaking about either.

The islands are all very beautiful and the people are all very friendly, but the sailors are beginning to wonder exactly where we are. Maps of the world show masses of islands off the coast of Asia, and the Admiral thinks we are sailing round these.

For the last few days the Indians with us have been talking about a big island they call Colba*. The Admiral has decided that this is Cipangu so that's where we're off to now.

28 October 1492 – *in the mouth of a river in the island of Juana (the Admiral has given Colba this name. Don't ask me why. I thought he thought it was Cipangu.)*

The Indians on board say this island has ten large rivers and is so big it takes more than twenty days to sail round it. That's why the Admiral is sure it's Cipangu, even though he's decided to give it another name.

Apparently the Indians are telling us there are gold mines here and places where they gather pearls on the seabed.

* *Cuba*

I can't make head or tail of what they are saying, but the Admiral thinks he can understand. From what they've told him, ships sail here from the Great Khan himself. They come to trade with a powerful king who reigns in this land. So it couldn't be anywhere but Cipangu, could it?

At last we can spend some time on shore. We're going to make camp here while we make contact with the king. There's a small village, very like ones we've seen on other islands, but the people had run away by the time we came ashore. That gave me the chance to have forty winks in one of their houses, and very comfortable it was too.

The houses aren't as solid as the ones at home. They have walls made of wood or canes bound close together. Thick palm leaves cover the tall roofs and from the outside they look like big tents. All the houses I've seen are clean and airy and what I really like are the beds. After sleeping on the open deck of the *Santa Maria* for more weeks than I like to remember, this is real luxury.

An Indian bed is unlike any bed I've ever seen. For a start it doesn't touch the ground. There isn't any sort of frame for a mattress either. In fact there isn't a mattress. You sort of sleep in the air, which sounds odd but is really comfortable when you get used to it (and when you finally get in). That's the only tricky thing about these Indian *hamaca** is climbing into them – it's the best way of describing going to bed.

* *hammock*

The *hamaca* is a like a large net, big enough to hold a man. It's tied by ropes at either end to two of the posts that hold up the roof. To go to sleep, you have to lower your body on to the net and then lie down. I worked this out after I'd fallen out a couple of times and got my hands and feet stuck through holes in the net like a fish. Once you're inside, though, it's brilliant. I had the best sleep since leaving Palos.

These *hamacas* would make great beds for sailors, because they wouldn't slide about like a solid bed, even if the ship moved from side to side. I reckon I'll take one home and show it around. I could be on to a winner with this.

29 October 1492 – *somewhere along the coast from where we were last night*

I'm glad I didn't take that *hamaca* I slept in. The Admiral gave me a real telling off when he found out I'd had a snooze in an Indian house. He's warned us not to steal or damage anything that belongs to the Indians.

I don't see how he squares these orders with keeping the Indians from San Salvador on board. But he's the Admiral and he knows best.

2 November 1492 – *further west along the coast*

Now the Admiral's decided that this isn't Cipangu after all. Apparently, it's the mainland of Cathay, the land of the Great Khan. In fact he has worked out that we are only a hundred leagues from Zayto and Quinsai, two of the great cities of Asia I remember from Master Isaac's maps.

This is why he sent the two officials from the Royal Court and Luis the interpreter to visit the local king. They have taken a letter from our King and Queen and samples of the spices we're looking for. With them are a couple of Indians and one of the sailors who knows all about expeditions like this, because he has been on several Portuguese voyages to the coast of Africa.

The Admiral has been to Africa too, and he expects to start trading with the Indies in the same way as the Portuguese trade in Africa. This must be the reason he's brought loads of the glass beads, hawks' bells and cheap cloth caps on the voyage. They're what the Portuguese use when they are trading in Africa.

I can't help thinking that there's something odd going on. Gifts like these are fine for people who don't have beads and bells, but surely the people of Cathay must have plenty of cheap things of their own? After all, they send us loads of valuables that are far more expensive than this stuff. If the Admiral expects to trade with the rich merchants of Cathay, why didn't he bring the sort of precious gifts that would interest them? I can't work this out.

6 November 1492 – *same place*

It looks as if we'll be on the move again before long. The men the Admiral sent to meet the king came back last night. They found a big village of about fifty huts, where the Indians gave them food and made them very welcome, but this wasn't the great city with fine buildings they were hoping for.

They did find something pretty crazy, though. They saw people doing the strangest thing with those dried leaves we keeping getting as presents. Men and women go around with a bunch of them in their hands, *on fire*! Not flaming hot, burn-your-hand fire, but burning just enough to send up a small cloud of smoke, which they breathe in for *enjoyment*!

Of all the amazing things we've come across, this has got to be the weirdest. I can see the Indian beds and boats, and the fruit and other foods we've discovered catching on at home – but these smoking leaves, no chance.

12 November 1492 – *somewhere off the coast of who knows where*

We've been in the Indies for exactly one month and, I have to say, they're nothing like the Indies I was expecting from reading Master Isaac's books.

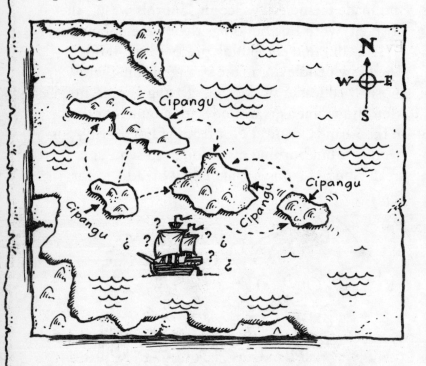

First we'd sailed past Cipangu. Then we'd found Cipangu. Then our Cipangu wasn't Cipangu, but, according to the Admiral, the mainland of Cathay. Now the Admiral thinks the mountains we're sailing past remind him of the island of Sicily in the Mediterranean!

We've found less gold than we'd come across in a market at home. The dogs don't bark. The meat the Indians like best comes from a strange-looking lizard*.

Even the plants which look like plants we know from Asia aren't the same. Yesterday I popped a fruit like a large strawberry into my mouth and my head nearly exploded. It was like eating fire. This pepper, or whatever it is, is hotter than anything I've ever tasted.

Now the Admiral is starting to talk about somewhere the Indians call Baneque. According to him, this is where gold can be found on the beach. He's convinced there's so much of it that people collect it at night in the sand by candlelight and then hammer it into bars.

I'll believe that when I see it.

* iguana

21 November 1492 – *off the coast again, not far from where we were ten days ago*

Everyone's feeling fed up. The winds have been against us, so we had to give up the idea of sailing south-eastwards to Baneque.

On all three ships, sailors have been asking what was going to happen next. And today, Martin Alonso Pinzon disobeyed the Admiral's orders and sailed away in the *Pinta*.

There was nothing the Admiral could do to stop him, but *caramba*, is he angry! I've heard him calling Captain Pinzon "greedy" under his breath. I think he's seriously worried that Captain Pinzon will find gold before he does and, worse still, will sail home ahead of us and claim that he's the first to discover the Indies. I wouldn't want to be in his place when the Admiral catches up with him.

23 November 1492 – *further along the coast from two days ago*

Just as things were looking as bad as they could be after Captain Pinzon left us, the Indians on board have begun telling us about a nearby island called Bohio. It seems that this is the home of a band of scary people who have one eye in the centre of their foreheads. They sound just like the Cyclops of ancient legends – the ones who captured sailors and ate them alive.

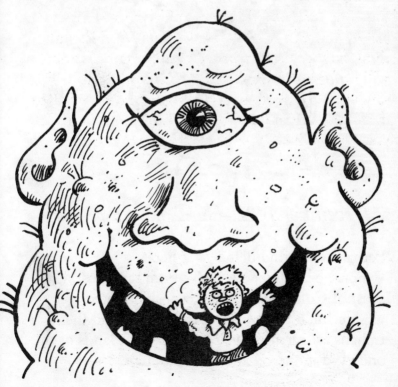

The Indians are also scared stiff of the people of Caniba, who they call Cannibals. They are very warlike and also eat their prisoners.

Out of the dozens of islands around here, wouldn't it be our luck to land up as some one-eyed monster's supper in Bohio, or be served as the main course to the people of Caniba?

7 December 1492 – *the island of Española**

Perhaps we'll find better luck here.

For the last ten days we've been sailing along the coast of Colba/Juana. The scenery has been wonderful, but we haven't found gold and the Indians are terrified we're going to the lands of the one-eyed monsters and the Cannibals.

* *Hispaniola*

However, the day before yesterday, we spotted land across the sea, sailed over to it and haven't spotted a monster or a Cannibal anywhere.

The scenery is different to the mountains and green forests on other islands. This land has open plains and hills like the ones in Spain, which is why the Admiral has decided to call it Española. We recognized oaks and strawberry plants like those at home.

We've caught skate and sole, just as we do around the Spanish coast, and the Admiral says he's even heard nightingales singing just like they do at home.

I wonder how much he knows about birds?

13 December 1492 – *Española*

Nine of us were sent ashore today to visit a large village inland. We found the village in a wide valley. There must be a thousand houses there, but all the people ran away when they saw us coming.

One of the Indians from the ship called them to come back, explaining that we wouldn't do them any harm, and soon we were surrounded by hundreds of people, patting us on the head, which is their way of being friendly. I wondered if I was supposed to bark in return?

The land around the village is very fertile and the people look well fed. They gave us a meal of fish and bread, though the bread tasted more like chestnuts than the wheat stuff we're used to at home. Whatever it is, it's a lot better than the biscuits on the ship.

We asked the Indians how the bread's made and they showed us something like a large carrot, which is grated into flour. As we liked it so much, they gave us some more to bring back to the ship.

Bread wasn't all we were given. Someone must have told them that the Admiral fancied the idea of taking some brightly coloured parrots back to Spain, and since we haven't much else to show for our voyage so far, many of the sailors decided they'd like parrots as well.

The Indians were so generous that before long we were surrounded by parrots, squawking, pecking and doing the other thing on our clothes which some people say is a sign of good luck.

I hope the Admiral is pleased with his feathered friends, because it's anyone's guess when we'll get home and he'll be spending a lot of time in their company.

Sailors having parrots as pets? Whatever next?!

Har-Har!

18 December 1492 – *along the coast of Española*

Only a week to go till Christmas, and we're getting into the party spirit on the *Santa Maria*.

There hasn't been much talk about the Great Khan for some time (I think the Admiral may be having second thoughts about where we are and whether the Great Khan fits into the picture at all). However, our luck took a turn for the better today when the Admiral was invited to meet the young king who reigns in this land.

He must only have been in his early twenties, like me, though he arrived with 200 attendants and was carried on a litter by four men. He may not have been wearing any clothes, but you could tell by the way his people treated him that he is as important to them as our King and Queen are to us.

The Admiral was dining in his cabin when the young king arrived, and he asked him inside for a bite to eat. I don't think King Ferdinand and Queen Isabella would have been too thrilled to be invited to tuck into four-month-old salt pork, old bean stew, dried fish and rock-hard sea biscuits, which have now got the added taste of weevils unless you remember to knock them out before taking a bite.

However, this young king politely had a mouthful of everything he was offered, said it was delicious (according to the Admiral) and then told his attendants to try some.

After they'd finished eating they exchanged gifts.
The King gave the Admiral a beautiful belt and two
pieces of gold (rather thin gold as far as I could see).
   In return the Admiral gave the King the cover
from his bed, which the King had taken a fancy to.

He also gave him the string of amber beads which he wore round his neck, a flask of orange-flavoured water and some red shoes – an odd selection, but the young King didn't seem to mind. In fact, a sailor who later saw his procession on the way back to his village told the Admiral that his gifts were carried in front of the king with great honour.

23 December 1492 – *further along the coast of Española*

Party on! I think I could get a taste for life aboard ship if it was always like this.

Española is a great place for a holiday. Maybe in the future people will sail here to spend the winter cruising past this wonderful tropical scenery over a clear blue sea, filled with brilliantly coloured fish. We've been to plenty of harbours where ships could anchor safely, and the people ashore are so friendly and generous, visitors would have a holiday of a lifetime. I'm glad we got here first.

Today we were the guests of another chieftain (possibly a king, it's hard to tell when everyone's dressed, or undressed, alike).

We were offered a new sort of bread which tastes delicious, even though it's made from a plant called *yucca*.

The Indians gave us a new type of fruit as well, covered in sharp prickles on the outside, but juicy and sweet inside. A sailor on the *Pinta* said it reminded him of an apple – I can't think why – and one of his friends said that the only sort of tree a prickly 'apple' like this could grow on was a pine tree. They thought that was terribly funny.

The Indians obviously wanted to make this a special outdoor party for us, because they cooked fish and lizards on the cooking frames I've noticed in other villages. These are made from poles tied together and raised above the ground, so that a fire can be lit underneath. You don't need pots and pans for this sort of cooking and because the food is cooked in the open, the smoke and smell don't bother you. In fact they made me feel even hungrier.

The Indians call this sort of cooking frame a *barbecua*. I mustn't confuse it with one of the *hamaca*. That could be seriously uncomfortable!

24 December 1492 – *Christmas Eve aboard the* Santa Maria, *sailing along the coast of Española*

After all the parties and feasting with the Indians along the coast, we're all in a very merry mood this Christmas Eve.

The Admiral doesn't normally sail at night because of the danger of running into rocks in the dark, but tonight the sea is calm, the sky is clear, we've raised a mug or two of wine to toast Their Majesties this Christmas and no-one seems to think there's any risk.

We had a bit of a singsong at sunset, to remind us of Christmas with the family and to stop us feeling homesick, since they're so far away. As well as the usual carols and Christmas songs, we made one up which was sung to a tune the sailors know about a piece of rigging called a 'one horse open sail' or something like that.

BEADS AND BELLS

Beads and bells, beads and bells,
Jingling every day,
We've brought beads and lots of bells
For the people of Cathay, hey!
Beads and bells, beads and bells,
Jingling every day,
The Portuguese sail eastwards,
But ours is a shorter way.

Crossing the Ocean Sea,
In a cramped and crowded ship,
We sailed to the unknown world,
On our historic trip,
Spices, gold and jewels,
Trade to make us rich,
These are what we came for –
But there has been a hitch, OH...

Beads and bells, beads and bells, etc.

Cipangu's roofs are gold
And silks the people wear,
But here the roofs are made of leaves
and the people go round bare.
They're friendly and they're kind,
They give us leaves and bread,
But we wish they'd trade with us
more precious things instead, OH...

Beads and bells, beads and bells, etc.

25 December 1492 – *Christmas Day, ashore on Española*

What a way to spend Christmas!

Yesterday evening we were sailing along part of the coast which had already been explored by boat. The sailors had told the Admiral that there were no dangerous rocks or reefs, so on we sailed into the night before Christmas.

Aboard ship everyone was feeling drowsy. The Admiral was asleep in his cabin. The ship's master was snoozing somewhere as well and I was peacefully dreaming of shepherds, a star, a stable and jingling beads and bells.

The next thing I knew, someone in my dream was shouting my name. "Look! Look!" one of the ship's boys was yelling.

This was followed by a grinding sound from the bottom of the ship, a judder and a crunch. Then the *Santa Maria* stopped moving.

Some of the sailors were already on their feet as I was rubbing my eyes. The door of the Admiral's cabin was flung open and people started shouting orders. It took a moment or two before I realized what had happened.

The boy who'd wakened us all was jabbering that it wasn't his fault. The sailor who should have been steering the ship had gone off for a nap and had told him to take the wheel (which is dead against the Admiral's orders). He hadn't seen the coral reef under the water, he wailed, and when the ship ran on to it all he could do was yell out in terror.

The Admiral ordered the boat over the side double-quick. The ship's master and the boat crew were told to take a rope and pull the ship off the reef into deeper water. At that time there wasn't much damage and, if we could refloat her, there was a chance of reaching shore and repairing her there.

Then we had our second stroke of bad luck. Instead of obeying the Admiral, the men in the boat rowed straight across to the *Niña*. They thought the *Santa Maria* was going down and they wanted to save their skins.

However, Captain Pinzon refused to let them aboard the *Niña* and sent them back to our ship. But by the time they returned, it was too late. The tide was running out.

The Admiral ordered the crew to cut down the mainmast and push it over the side, to make the ship lighter, but by now the *Santa Maria* had settled onto the reef, the bottom boards had burst open and water was flooding into the hold.

We were shipwrecked and our merry Christmas vanished like my dream.

The largest of our ships will never float again. Another disappeared over a month ago. Now all we have is the smallest of the three.

How were we all going to get home? That was my first thought.

Luckily the sea stayed calm, and as daylight came, we started unloading all the stores from the *Santa Maria* into the two boats to take them ashore.

This was when the Indians who live nearby arrived to lend a hand. King Guacanagari sent big canoes to help rescue our belongings. He gave us houses in which we could store our food and gear and the Indians haven't taken as much as a grain of pepper the whole time.

So that's how we spent Christmas, in a house surrounded by piles of food and gifts. Terrific – I don't think!

26 December 1492 – *ashore on Española, in the land of King Guacanagari*

I've got to hand it to the Admiral. Somehow he sees the bright side of even the biggest disaster.

Today he told us that the shipwreck was a sign from God that he should make a settlement here and start trading with the King.

He's also had a brainwave – we can break up the *Santa Maria* and use the wood from her to build a fort.

There was another part of his brainwave – some of the crew could stay behind, while the rest of us sailed home. He'd be back, the Admiral assured everyone, and those left behind would have a great time here, a sort of extended holiday.

27 December 1492 – *in the land of King Guacanagari*

Work's going well on building the fort.

There's been more good news too. Indians have seen our missing ship, the *Pinta*, somewhere along the coast to the east. The King has sent a canoe with one of our sailors to find her and order Captain Martin Alonso Pinzon to sail here to join us.

I don't suppose he'll be in much of a hurry to do that.

1 January 1493 – *New Year's Day, in the land of King Guacanagari*

A year ago I was enjoying life back in Toledo with Master Isaac and his family. What a lot can happen in twelve months!

Anyhow, the Admiral's talking about going home now that the *Santa Maria's* been wrecked. If my luck holds, I could be back in Spain by the spring.

I'm not volunteering to stay behind – no way. But I'm amazed how many men have jumped at the chance. Do they know something I don't about the voyage home?

Nearly forty of them will be remaining in La Navidad – that's the name the Admiral has given to our first settlement in these new lands. He's called it that because the settlement was 'born' as a result of the shipwreck on Jesus's Nativity, Christmas Day.

Even though the Indians are friendly at the moment, the Admiral isn't taking any chances. He ordered one of our cannons to shoot a big hole through the wreck of the *Santa Maria*, to show what Spanish weapons can do.

He also impressed the King and his people with the top-notch bows and swords he's leaving behind. If there's any trouble, the men in La Navidad will be able to look after themselves.

6 January 1493 – *anchored off Española, eastwards of La Navidad*

We sailed away from La Navidad two days ago, after saying goodbye to our shipmates and King Guacanagari and his people.

I was up in the rigging on lookout duty, thinking this through, when a sail appeared in the distance and started to grow bigger. It was the *Pinta*, sailing towards us after disappearing over six weeks ago!

She was alongside before nightfall and we anchored together. The Admiral was hopping mad when Captain Pinzon came aboard the *Niña*, but he did his best to keep his temper.

Captain Pinzon made some excuses for sailing away like that, but you could tell the Admiral thought it was his greed which had made him take off. From what he told the Admiral, he's had more luck finding gold than we have. I don't suppose that news went down very well.

8 January 1493 – *off the coast of Española*

We've spent the last two days exploring the coast. Now that the *Pinta* is back with us once again, the Admiral is keener to explore these lands a little more before we set sail for home. Could Captain Pinzon's story of trading a lot of gold with Indians along the coast have anything to do with it?

Today we took on supplies of wood and fresh water to prepare for the voyage back to Spain. We found water in a large river and while we were resting between boatloads, we noticed grains of gold lying in the sand. Later, grains of gold were found stuck in the metal hoops of the buckets and casks. The Admiral named the river the *Rio del Oro**. Well, wouldn't you?

It's funny how life works out. Here we are, spending nearly three months wandering around these islands looking for gold without much to show for it, and just as we're about to head for home, we find a river so full of the stuff we'll be almost drinking it all the way back across the Ocean Sea.

* *River of Gold*

13 January 1493 – *still off the coast of Española*

After today most of us have had enough discovering for the time being.

It began like most other days we've had since we arrived in these islands. We anchored off yet *another* beach of beautiful golden sand, and a party went ashore in the boat to find *ajes**, which Indians have given us to eat when we've visited their villages.

On the beach the sailors started talking to a group of Indian men, who looked fiercer and more warlike than any we have met so far. Their faces were smeared with charcoal and their long hair hung down their backs, tied at the end with birds' feathers.

The Admiral thought these might be the Cannibal Indians, we had heard about back along the coast, and he invited one of them on to the *Niña* to talk to him.

* sweet potatoes

The Indian mentioned an island rich in gold (haven't I heard that somewhere already on this voyage?). And he spoke about another inhabited only by women.

I reckon he was pulling our legs, but he was given something to eat before being taken ashore with presents of coloured cloth and glass beads. So far, so good.

On the beach, our men started trading with the Indians, exchanging beads and bells, cloth and caps for the bows and arrows they were carrying. These are the first weapons we have seen since we landed in October, and they're as big as the ones used in France and England.

After two bows had been bought, the Indians had second thoughts, because they picked up their weapons and threatened to attack our men. You should never insult a man with feathers in his hair, I always say.

Several of the sailors were armed and ready, as the Admiral had commanded throughout the voyage, so they were able to drive the Indians away. Two were injured, but the rest escaped unharmed.

Now we know that not all the Indians are friendly. It's disappointing, but I suppose if the Indians had crossed the Ocean Sea and 'discovered' *us*, they would have found that people in Europe can be just the same – both murderous *and* matey.

16 January 1493 – *at sea, on our way home!*

Those Indians we had the fight with a couple of days ago must have got the Admiral thinking about the island filled with women, because he decided to make a final visit there before setting off across the Ocean Sea to Spain.

No-one else was that excited by the idea, which shows how keen everyone is to get back home. But the Admiral was having none of it.

However, this time Fate was on *our* side, and instead of blowing us in the direction of the all-woman island, the winds swung round and blew in the direction of Spain.

Our ships are no good at sailing straight into the wind, and it wasn't long before the Admiral gave the order to change course. The *Niña* and the *Pinta* swung round and pointed their bows to the north-east by east.

¡Viva España! Home, here we come!

25 January 1493 – *somewhere on the Ocean Sea*

I'd forgotten how boring sailing can be when you're out of the sight of land. I miss the extra space we had on the *Santa Maria* as well.

We're not sailing home as fast as we sailed away from it. After the first day the winds turned against us and we made slow progress.

In the end the Admiral took us further north and we started picking up winds blowing from the west. These are the ones we need if we are going to sail home safely. I hope they keep up.

The food wasn't up to much on the voyage out, but now it's worse than ever. After the fight with the Indians, we left Española sharpish and before we'd loaded all the supplies we needed. Now we've got sea biscuits, those Indian vegetables called *ajes* and wine. That's about it.

Luckily it's been calm enough to fish, and today we caught a dolphin and a very big shark, which will give us something tasty for a few days. I don't mind saying I really fancy a nice piece of lizard cooked on a *barbecua*, followed by one of those pine-apple fruits.

10 February 1493 – somewhere on the moon (well, it's more interesting than writing "somewhere on the Ocean Sea"…)

There hasn't been much to write about in the last two weeks. Either the Admiral is on a lucky streak or he knows more about the Ocean Sea than he's letting on. Whichever it is, the wind keeps blowing us eastwards day after day. The sea has stayed calm and the weather is more like spring at home than the middle of February.

I should be pleased about all of this, and I would be, if I felt sure that anyone on the voyage knew where we are.

Take today, for instance. Captain Pinzon on our ship, the *Niña*, and his two navigators have calculated that we have now sailed beyond the Azores, the islands in the Ocean Sea which belong to the King of Portugal. The Admiral, on the other hand, is sure that we are still west of the Azores. So he makes our position over a hundred leagues behind the other three. With food running low, that's great news.

12 February 1493 – somewhere on the top of some big waves on the Ocean Sea

I had a hunch the good weather couldn't last, and it hasn't. The sky turned stormy today, the sea grew rough, and the Admiral could be heard muttering about the shipwrights in Palos and hoping they'd done a good job in preparing our ships for this voyage.

I decided to pass on the daily meal – I've not been feeling too good today.

13 February 1493 – *somewhere in a storm on the Ocean Sea*

The wind is so strong and the sea so wild that the sails were lowered last night and we were blown along with bare masts.

Now the wind has grown even stronger. The waves are so high we lose sight of the *Pinta* when they rise above us. Last week I was bored with looking at flat, calm water, day after day. Now I'm terrified we may end up at the bottom of the Ocean Sea, not on the other side of it.

One day, Luc, you'll learn to recognize your luck.

14 February 1493 – *still in the storm on the Ocean Sea (but for how much longer?)*

God must have been angry with us today. He threw such a storm upon our ships that the sea crashed together in huge waves which broke over us time after time.

The *Pinta* tried to stay close to the *Niña*, but the wind was so strong she could no longer hold her course and was blown from our sight, leaving us alone in this king of storms.

Our ship was being tossed from wave to wave because there was not enough weight in the hold to keep her steady. We left so many of our stores with our shipmates at La Navidad that the ship needed rocks to replace them, to keep the balance right. The fight with the Cannibal Indians prevented us loading these, and we set sail without proper ballast. Now, in the middle of this terrible storm, we have filled empty barrels with sea water, which seems a strange thing to do, but does make the ship feel more stable.

The Admiral called us all together and ordered a lottery to seek God's help (it was his way of keeping up our spirits). We didn't use tickets or numbers. Chickpeas were put into a bag, one of which was marked with knife cuts in the form of a cross. It was agreed that whoever drew the marked chickpea would make a pilgrimage to the monastery of Guadalupe in western Spain, to thank God for our safe return home.

Then the Admiral made the first draw and picked the marked chickpea. It wasn't us – it was him. Funny that.

Another lottery for another pilgrimage was drawn, and when a sailor picked the marked chickpea, the Admiral promised to pay his travel expenses.

The Admiral drew the marked chickpea for the third lottery (anything fishy about this?) and then we all vowed that when we reach land we will go in our shirtsleeves to the first shrine to Saint Mary, Mother of God, to give her our thanks.

Having something to look forward to cheered us up a bit. Though while we tried to hide from the waves, the Admiral was in his cabin writing furiously on a sheet of parchment. Later he called me to him, to ask for a piece of waterproof, waxed cloth and a wooden barrel.

The sailors thought he was sending another plea to God to save us, but I caught sight of what he had written. It was a letter to Their Majesties, telling them of all the things we have seen and discovered in the Indies. The letter was wrapped in the cloth, sealed inside the barrel and thrown over the side of the ship.

The Admiral must be thinking that our ship might sink. If it does, Captain Pinzon could claim the glory for discovering our route to the Indies – unless someone finds the Admiral's letter in the barrel and delivers it to the King and Queen.

I haven't told anyone else about this, but I don't feel much like eating – even if it could be my last meal this side of Paradise.

15 February 1493 – *off the islands of the Azores (we think)*

God has answered our prayers – Paradise will have to wait many years for me to arrive, I hope!
Land came into sight after sunrise and although we don't know for sure what land it is, the Admiral insists that it is part of the King of Portugal's Azores and that his navigation was right all along.

19 February 1493 – *the island of Santa Maria, in the Azores*

I don't think I will ever be so pleased again to step on to dry land! It took us two days to reach harbour because the winds were against us, and the people of the island tell us that it is a miracle we have survived. The storms this winter have been the worst anyone can remember.

Yesterday evening, food and water was sent to our ship by the captain of the island, with a message that he would visit us today. So, this morning the Admiral sent half the crew ashore, in their shirtsleeves as we had vowed, to give thanks for our safe arrival in the first church of Saint Mary they found. The other half of the crew were going to make the same pilgrimage when the first lot returned.

However, they didn't return. Despite his welcome yesterday, the captain of the island has taken them prisoner and now threatens the rest of us. Thank you very much.

He doesn't believe that we have been to the Indies at all. He suspects we have been trading in Africa, in lands controlled by the King of Portugal.

What a homecoming – and this is supposed to be civilization!

24 February 1493 – *at sea once more, on our way home (I hope)*

It's taken five days to get away from the Portuguese on Santa Maria.

After the captain of the island captured half the crew, the Admiral hauled up the anchor and put out to sea. But with only three proper sailors on board and bad weather, we had to return two days later.

In the meantime, the captain of the island had calmed down. He sent his officers to the ship to look at the official papers given to the Admiral by our King and Queen. These did the trick, and the prisoners were released and allowed to row back to the *Niña*.

We didn't waste time in getting away. The winds were against us at first, but now they are behind us and we are sailing for the coast of Spain – better luck this time.

3 March 1493 – *somewhere on the Ocean Sea (still no sign of home)*

When I think what an easy voyage we had to the Indies last autumn, it's almost as if God doesn't want us to reach Spain alive.

Another storm has fallen on us since we set sail from Santa Maria, and today the winds hit the ship with such force that the sails were nearly ripped from the masts. The Admiral decided it was time for another chickpea lottery for a shirtsleeved pilgrimage. He won again, the cheat.

To show God that we're really serious about getting home safely, we all agreed we'd fast on bread and water the first Saturday after we reach land. You can't say fairer than that after weeks of living on seven-month-old sea biscuits and Indian vegetables.

God wasn't that impressed, however. All day long, the storm blew us furiously before it, without a stitch of sail on the masts. Rain lashed down and lighting burst from the heavens.

Only at dusk did we see signs of forgiveness. Through the clouds we caught sight of land, but it's too dangerous to approach. We have wait on the storm-tossed sea until first light tomorrow to find out where we are now.

4 March 1493 – *at anchor in the River Tagus, in Portugal (wouldn't you know it!)*

Of all the places to have ended up along the coast, the storm has blown us right into the outer harbour of Lisbon, the capital of Portugal.

The Admiral has written a letter to the King of Portugal, asking permission to enter the main harbour. He has told him that we have come from the Indies, not from Africa.

I don't know how the King of Portugal is going to take this news, since he and his experts turned down the Admiral's idea several years ago.

We'll have to hope for the best.

5 March 1493 – *at anchor in the River Tagus*

It looks as if things have worked out all right.

The master of the King of Portugal's great ship, which is anchored close by, came to the *Niña* today demanding to know where we have sailed from.

The Admiral said that he was the Admiral of the Sovereigns of Spain and didn't have to explain anything to anyone except them.

The Portuguese master didn't like this, but he kept his cool and asked if he could see the letters from our King and Queen.

It all got a bit out of hand, actually.

The Royal letters did the trick in the end. Before long, boats were approaching us with drums and trumpets playing, and now the Portuguese are offering to give us anything we need. All because we have sailed to the Indies by going westwards – and sailed back again.

Good old Admiral Colón. It's taken him years to pull it off, but now there's no mistaking what he's done. He's won his place in history!

This is what it must feel like to be famous.

13 March 1493 – *at sea, on the last leg home*

There'll be no stopping the Admiral now. The last week has been amazing and we haven't even reached Spain yet.

Every day fleets of boats filled with people have visited us to bring gifts and greetings. They're calling us heroes for winning these new lands for Our Lord. I think they're also fascinated to see all the other new things we've brought back with us, especially the Indians and the parrots. Don't know which they find more amazing, actually.

The King of Portugal summoned the Admiral to visit him a few days ago, and he only returned from the royal palace last night. The meeting went fine, once it was clear that we had been to the Indies and not to Africa – though I bet the King of Portugal is secretly kicking himself for turning down the chance to add our lands in the Indies to his kingdom.

He offered the Admiral horses, so that he could finish his journey to our King and Queen overland, but the Admiral preferred to return to the ship. I think he feels safer at sea. After the storm, I can't imagine why.

While he was away, we repaired the ship as best we could and took on supplies for the last part of the voyage, so that we could leave with this morning's tide.

If the weather holds, we'll be home the day after tomorrow!

15 March 1493 – *Palos, home at last!*

At midday, we sailed into Palos on the rising tide.

The Enterprise of the Indies is over. We've proved the doubters wrong. There is a way to reach land by sailing west – and we've done it.

"Did you win any souls for Our Lord?" shouted the monk who'd seen me off seven months ago.

"You could say that," I called back.

When I was ashore, the first place I went was the church of St George, where this whole adventure began. I promised God I'd try to be a better Christian. It seemed the best way of thanking him for bringing me safely home.

The *Niña* wasn't the only ship to sail into Palos today. A few hours after we dropped anchor, the *Pinta* arrived home too. The storm in the Ocean Sea had driven her far to the north of Spain and it's taken all this time to sail south to Palos.

I didn't see Captain Martin Alonso Pinzon go ashore. I heard he went straight home, looking pale and ill*. I bet they'll still be talking about the Admiral in centuries to come, but will anyone remember Captain Pinzon? I wonder.

* *Pinzon died shortly afterwards*

News of our return has spread quickly through Palos, and people keep stopping me to ask in amazement, "Is it true where you've sailed to?"

"Yes," I tell them, and leave it at that.

The truth is, I've no idea where we've been and nor does anyone else – not even the Admiral.

He's talking about sailing off again later this year, but I'm done with discovering. You won't catch me disappearing over the horizon again for a *long* time, not even if Their Majesties give me a first-class ticket to America.

THE REST OF THE STORY

Luc Landahoya's diary ends at the same point as Christopher Columbus's own journal. However, we know from other historical records that Columbus's triumph was celebrated for months afterwards.

King Ferdinand and Queen Isabella gave him a hero's welcome after he travelled across Spain to their court in Barcelona. They marvelled at the Indians who accompanied him, and at the parrots, the strange new fruits and vegetables, and everything else brought back from the Enterprise of the Indies.

Columbus was given new titles and honours. He had a coat of arms and now became a nobleman.

News of his discovery spread far and fast. Within two months of his return, every important city in Europe had heard about the voyage. The printed version of the story did become a bestseller, just as Columbus hoped it would. By the end of the year, copies were available in several languages throughout Europe.

Sadly for Columbus, he never enjoyed such popularity and praise again. He made three more voyages to discover lands in the west and build settlements there, but these could not hope to repeat the success of his first voyage. There were long-running arguments with fellow explorers, trouble with the Indians and growing doubts among some people as to whether or not he had sailed to Asia, as he claimed.

In the end, even Ferdinand and Isabella had lost their early enthusiasm for his expeditions. Outside his family, few people showed much interest when Christopher Columbus died in May 1506.

PUBLISHER'S ADDENDUM

While it is true that many of the names and events mentioned in this diary are the same as those in better known accounts of Columbus's first voyage, we now have serious doubts about what is printed here.

We have tried to make contact with the two so-called experts who told Mr Dickinson (after he had paid them) that the diary had really been written by a crew member of the *Santa Maria* in 1492.

We must now report that neither Dr Miles Away nor Don Believavor D'Ovid can be traced, through the Internet or any other means. It looks as if they were fakes, as does the diary.

Almost everyone who sailed with Columbus in 1492 has been identified, and none of them had the unlikely name of Luc Landahoya.

There are no records either of anyone called Isaac Palestino living and teaching in Toledo at the end of the fifteenth century, though it is true that Jews and Muslims were forced to leave Spain at the times mentioned.

Perhaps the most important proof that this diary is false lies in the last word of the last sentence, when the diarist uses the name 'America'. No-one writing in 1493 would have ever heard land on the other side of the Atlantic called America. We now know that the islands Columbus sailed to in 1492 lie in the Caribbean. 'America' was not called America until 1507, the year after Columbus died.

Lastly, we should not forget the first date in the diary. Could this be the final clue?

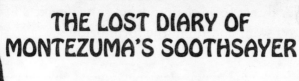

Order Form

To order direct from the publishers, just make a list of the titles you want and fill in the form below:

Name ....

Address ....

....

....

Send to: Dept 6, HarperCollins Publishers Ltd, Westerhill Road, Bishopbriggs, Glasgow G64 2QT.

Please enclose a cheque or postal order to the value of the cover price, plus:

UK & BFPO: Add £1.00 for the first book, and 25p per copy for each additional book ordered.

Overseas and Eire: Add £2.95 service charge. Books will be sent by surface mail but quotes for airmail despatch will be given on request.

A 24-hour telephone ordering service is available to holders of Visa, MasterCard, Amex or Switch cards on 0141- 772 2281.

Collins
An *Imprint* of HarperCollins*Publishers*